THE HEY HEY MAN

by Sid Fleischman

Illustrated by Nadine Bernard Westcott

An Atlantic Monthly Press Book
Little, Brown and Company
BOSTON　　　　TORONTO

Books by Sid Fleischman

Mr. Mysterious & Company	*The Ghost on Saturday Night*
By the Great Horn Spoon!	*Mr. Mysterious's Secrets of Magic*
The Ghost in the Noonday Sun	*McBroom Tells a Lie*
Chancy and the Grand Rascal	*Me and the Man on the Moon-Eyed Horse*
Longbeard the Wizard	*McBroom and the Beanstalk*
Jingo Django	*Humbug Mountain*
The Wooden Cat Man	*The Hey Hey Man*

FIRST EDITION

Library of Congress Cataloging in Publication Data

Fleischman, Albert Sidney.
　The Hey Hey man.

　"An Atlantic Monthly Press book."
　SUMMARY: A thief steals a farmer's gold but is outwitted by a mischievous wood spirit—the Hey Hey Man.
　[1. Robbers and outlaws—Fiction] I. Westcott, Nadine Bernard. II. Title.
PZ7.F5992He　　[E]　　78-31702
ISBN 0-316-26001-0

ATLANTIC—LITTLE, BROWN BOOKS
ARE PUBLISHED BY
LITTLE, BROWN AND COMPANY
IN ASSOCIATION WITH
THE ATLANTIC MONTHLY PRESS

*Published simultaneously in Canada
by Little, Brown & Company (Canada) Limited*

PRINTED IN THE UNITED STATES OF AMERICA

For Lydia
in memory of Don

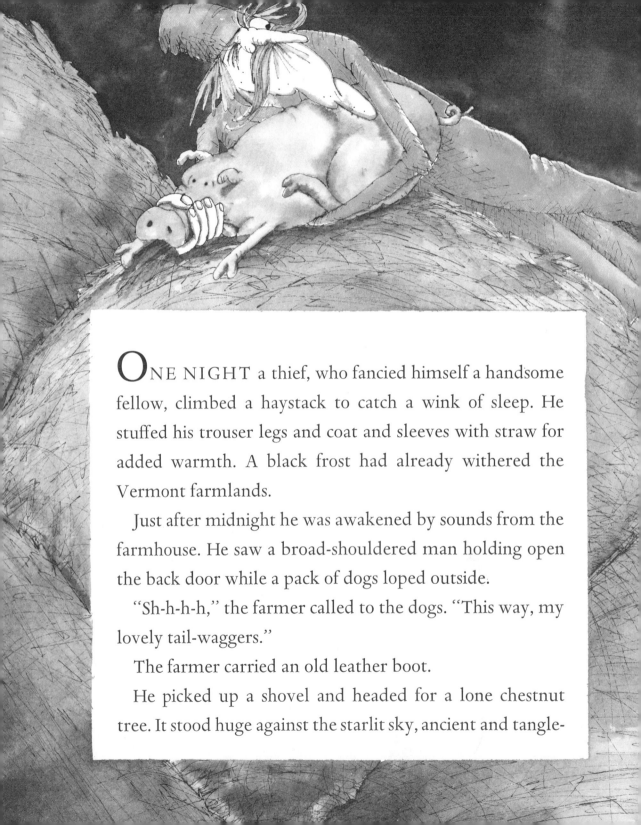

ONE NIGHT a thief, who fancied himself a handsome fellow, climbed a haystack to catch a wink of sleep. He stuffed his trouser legs and coat and sleeves with straw for added warmth. A black frost had already withered the Vermont farmlands.

Just after midnight he was awakened by sounds from the farmhouse. He saw a broad-shouldered man holding open the back door while a pack of dogs loped outside.

"Sh-h-h-h," the farmer called to the dogs. "This way, my lovely tail-waggers."

The farmer carried an old leather boot.

He picked up a shovel and headed for a lone chestnut tree. It stood huge against the starlit sky, ancient and tangle-

branched. The seedling had come from the Old Country, and for generations folks had pointed it out as the Hey Hey Tree.

Some believed that a prankish tree spirit, a Hey Hey Man, had crossed the ocean with it.

At the base of the tree the farmer set the boot on the ground. He began to dig, then stopped. He peered up into the limbs and branches.

"Hey Hey Man," he called softly. "You up there, neighbor? Give us a peek at you."

The tree stood in stately silence.

"A shy one, you are," said the farmer, with a chuckle. "Or no one at all. Granny tales. How come my hounds can't sniff you out? Still, if you're watching, don't make off with my hard-earned savings, or I'll chop down your tree. No, I've nothing to fear from you, Mr. Hey Hey Man."

He finished digging the hole and turned to his dogs. "Put your noses to the boot. Don't forget the scent, my dear ankle-biters."

The dogs snuffed and sniffed the old jackboot, their tails whipping the chill air.

The farmer dropped the boot into the hole. It landed with a rattle of coins, and he covered it over with dirt and fallen leaves. "Come along, my pot-lickers," he said. "Before long the ground will freeze solid as rock. The gold'll be safe all winter."

The farmer and the dogs returned to the warmth of the house.

"What luck!" the thief muttered, laughing to himself. "A boot full of valuables, and not a single dog to guard it. The jabbering fool lets the old fleabags sleep with him!"

He rose from the haystack. Silent as a cat, step by step, he made for the chestnut tree. He dug up the jackboot, filled in the hole, and covered it again with leaves. Then,

with the boot heaved over one shoulder, he moved as quietly as a shadow across the meadow.

Finally he began to run. With his clothing stuffed with straw he thought he must look like a scarecrow come to life. But soon, with treasure to spend, he'd be wearing ruffled shirts and velvet coats. What a dashing figure he'd cut!

He leaped a stone wall and sat down to catch his breath. For the first time, he reached into the boot, clutched up some coins, and examined them in the cold starlight. They shone like a handful of embers, and he yipped out a short, joyous laugh.

But the laughter caught in his throat. There on the wall stood a banty little man. He wore short leather breeches, green woolen knee socks, and an Alpine hat with a sprig of chestnut leaves tucked into the band.

"A chill in the air tonight," the man said pleasantly. He clutched a small whip under his arm.

"Stand where you are!" the thief shouted.

The little man clinked a few coins in his hands. "Yours? Yes, I think you must be dropping gold pieces like grain from a torn sack."

The thief looked at the sole of the jackboot. The farmer had worn a hole in it.

"I declare!" the little man remarked. "Is that Anton's old boot? I've seen it on his foot for many a year."

"One boot looks like another," the thief snapped. "Hand over my gold pieces."

"A pleasure," the man said, and poured the coins into the thief's palm.

11

Then the thief reached inside his sleeve for a wad of straw and plugged the hole in the boot.

"I'll walk with you for a piece," said the man.

The thief scowled. "I travel alone, stranger."

"As you wish."

And the thief took off toward the woods. He rushed along, deeper and deeper into the forest. By the time dawn broke, he couldn't find his way out.

And there, in the gray gloom, on a fallen log, sat the banty little man with chestnut leaves stuck in his hat.

"How did you get here?" the thief shouted. "Stop following me!"

"Only trying to be of service. You're lost, I see."

The thief's eyes darkened. "Where did you come from? Who are you?"

"Think of me as your obedient servant—the Hey Hey Man."

"Never heard of you!"

"It doesn't matter. You've been walking in circles. Never

find your way out of the forest unless you follow your nose.
That's my advice, sir. Follow your nose."

"Numbskull!" thundered the thief. "I can't see my nose
to follow it."

"I can fix that," remarked the little man. He cracked his
whip and said, "Hey! Hey!"

The thief's nose grew out as long and lumpy as a horse-
radish root.

"Always glad to oblige," said the Hey Hey Man amiably.

"Confound you!"

But the Hey Hey Man had vanished into the deep forest
shadows.

The thief followed the end of his nose, like the jack staff
of a ship, and it led him out of the woods.

He came to an unplowed cornfield and stopped to rest. "No need to footrace it," he told himself. "It'll be spring before the farmer and his curs discover the boot missing."

The dry cornstalks scraped and rustled in the wind. And there stood the Hey Hey Man with the whip under his arm.

"Temperature's dropping fast," he said.

The thief jumped to his feet, and his eyes shot fire. "You cussed little mongrel! Look at this tarnatious nose! Who are you? The devil?"

"No relation," said the Hey Hey Man.

"I'll maul the pinfeathers out of you!"

"No time, sir, no time." The Hey Hey Man cocked an ear. "Hear that? Listen."

"To what?"

"A pack of dogs. Sounds like they're on the hunt."

"Moonshine!" snarled the thief. "I don't hear a thing!"

"I declare!" remarked the little man. "Well, I can fix that." He cracked his whip and said, "Hey! Hey!"

Instantly the thief's ears grew as big as cabbage leaves.

The thief could now hear the distant baying of dogs. He turned dishwater-pale.

He fixed blazing eyes on the Hey Hey Man. "Blast your pesky hide! You didn't fetch me all the gold pieces!"

"I may have missed a few in the dark."

The thief picked up the jackboot and began to run. No doubt the farmer had found a trail of coins on the ground, discovered that the hole was empty, and turned his curs loose.

The thief went crashing through the dry cornstalks and came to a clearing. The bark and blather of the hounds was getting closer.

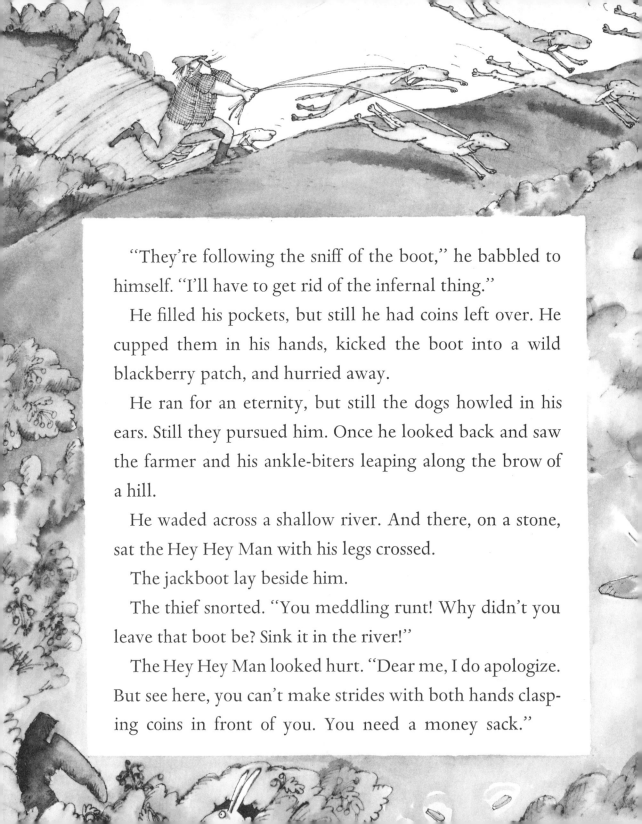

"They're following the sniff of the boot," he babbled to himself. "I'll have to get rid of the infernal thing."

He filled his pockets, but still he had coins left over. He cupped them in his hands, kicked the boot into a wild blackberry patch, and hurried away.

He ran for an eternity, but still the dogs howled in his ears. Still they pursued him. Once he looked back and saw the farmer and his ankle-biters leaping along the brow of a hill.

He waded across a shallow river. And there, on a stone, sat the Hey Hey Man with his legs crossed.

The jackboot lay beside him.

The thief snorted. "You meddling runt! Why didn't you leave that boot be? Sink it in the river!"

The Hey Hey Man looked hurt. "Dear me, I do apologize. But see here, you can't make strides with both hands clasping coins in front of you. You need a money sack."

He cracked his whip and said, "Hey! Hey!"

The jackboot turned into a cloth sack.

"Hang your sack!" the thief exclaimed. "What I need is a horse!"

"Wish I could oblige," said the Hey Hey Man. "But I need straw to make a horse. No, I can't help you there."

The thief's eyes lit up. "Straw! How do you think I've kept from freezing?"

He poured the coins from his hands into the sack. Then he shook his sleeves and straw fell to the ground. He pulled straw from inside his trouser legs. He plucked straw from all his clothing and threw it on the pile.

"Yes, that might do," remarked the Hey Hey Man.

"Hurry!" The thief could hear the hounds snorting. They'd soon be at his ankles. He emptied the gold from his pockets into the cloth sack and knotted the top.

The Hey Hey Man circled the pile of straw. He peered thoughtfully at it. Then he cracked his whip and said, "Hey! Hey!"

And there, nostrils breathing steam, stood a chestnut mare.

The thief jumped onto her back and rode away.

The horse galloped wildly across the countryside. She raced under the boughs of trees and the thief ducked low on her back. He held on for dear life. There was no holding or turning the beast.

She rattled along a pasture, over a covered bridge, and along a field. The wind blinded the thief. It whistled past his ears and turned his nose red.

The thief felt frozen to the bone. But he didn't care. Let the horse have her head, he thought. She was whisking him miles and miles from the farmer's tail-wagging, ankle-biting hounds.

Suddenly the mare hauled up short. The thief flew over her neck and into a stack of hay.

Still clutching the sack of gold he looked up. He saw a farmhouse, and not far off, a chestnut tree.

On a lower limb sat the Hey Hey Man.

"I'm back where I started!" the thief cried out.

"You gave that galloping haystack her head," remarked

the Hey Hey Man. "A horse always returns to the stable, so to speak."

The thief was shaking with anger and shivering with cold. "I'm off!" he chattered. "And keep out of my sight, I warn you!"

"But you're chilled to the bone." He cracked his whip and said, "Hey! Hey!"

A fire blazed up not far from where the thief stood.

"Warm yourself first," said the Hey Hey Man, putting away his whip.

The thief tried but couldn't resist the fire. He beat his arms and held out his hands to the flames. The tip of his nose began to scorch, and he reared back. What *did* he look like? Nearby stood a water trough, and the thief caught a first and awful glimpse of himself.

"I'm uglified!" he roared. "Look what you've done to me! My nose! My ears! Uglier'n mud! Uglier'n sin! I'll be recognized wherever I go!"

The Hey Hey Man sighed. "I was only trying to be of service."

"Idiot! I'll have to hide myself away in the mountains!"

"I expect so. But nothing to worry about. Seven years and the spell will pass."

"Seven years!" bellowed the thief. "You've the power—do something now!"

The man in the tree shrugged. "It's not so easy to undo the handiwork of a Hey Hey Man, sir. You would have to pass a test."

"What test? Get on with it!"

The banty little man scratched his chin. "Ah! I have it. Watch the bag. I'll go for a stroll. If everything you find in the bag is still there when I return, you pass the test."

"Go for the stroll," the thief laughed. "What a simple-minded test," he thought.

"Hey! Hey!" whispered the little man, with a soft snap of his whip, as he wandered off for a stroll.

The thief resumed rubbing his hands over the fire, and kept a sharp eye on the sack of coins. "But what if the farmer should return?" he thought. "I'd better move it out of clear sight."

When the thief lifted the sack it felt as light as air.

Surprise choked his breath. Quickly he opened the sack. It was full of fleas.

A groan of anguish burst from his lips. "Tricked! A sackful of fleas! That runt has *hey-heyed* the gold into vermin!"

The thief stood dazed. But when the fleas began leaping
out of the sack he came to his senses. The test. He must not
let a single jumper get away!

He fell to his hands and knees and pursued the insects.

For every flea he captured, six others hopped away. He dove here and scrambled there, and began muttering to himself.

He lost track of time, and before long he was yelling out like a madman. "Got you! There's another! Hold still, you bloodsucking speck of nothing."

Suddenly he became aware of the farmer's voice.

"How do, stranger? Lose your watch or something? I declare if you don't look like a pig rooting in a potato patch."

The dogs loped forward and the thief reared back. "Hold your dogs!"

"My tail-waggers won't harm you," said the farmer.

The thief attempted to conceal his face behind his arm. "Fleas! They'll pick up fleas!"

"Won't be the first time," said the farmer. "You didn't notice a rascal about carrying an old jackboot, did you?"

"No," answered the thief, his voice muffled. By now, he knew, fleas were hopping far and wide. There'd be no re-filling the sack with them. He was beaten.

"Our life savings gone, me and the dogs," said the farmer. "Do hate to think it was the little chunk of a man. Never heard that thievery was his line of trade. But my hounds would have caught anyone else." He looked up sadly at the Hey Hey Tree. It would pain him to chop it down. But all he had left of value was the lumber in it. "Might as well fetch my ax."

"I'll be on my way," said the thief.

"Stick to the main road," advised the farmer. "Otherwise you might meet up with a pint-size feller in leather breeches. Be on your guard. Infernally clever, that one. He leads travelers astray. Full of mischief."

The thief groaned and slouched away, still concealing his face.

The farmer went to the shed for a heavy ax and the dogs sniffed the sack and the ground around it. While he was gone, the stillness was broken by the snap of a whip and a whisper.

"Hey! Hey!"

The farmer returned to the chestnut tree and lifted his ax. He checked his swing in midair.

The dogs had begun to scratch themselves in a sudden, itching fury. The entire pack. Paws scraped away at necks and chins and chests. They nipped at their backs.

The farmer watched in bafflement. "As I'm alive!" he exclaimed. "My dear tail-waggers!"

31

It was hard to believe his own eyes.

The dogs were scratching and nipping gold pieces out of their fur. They were shedding coins as if they were fleas.